The Longest, Strongest Thread

For my grandma, with love

2022 First US edition
Text and illustrations copyright © Inbal Leitner, 2020

First published in Great Britain in 2020 by Scallywag
Press Ltd., 10 Sutherland Row, London SW1V 4JT

Published by Charlesbridge
9 Galen Street • Watertown, MA 02472
(617) 926-0329 • www.charlesbridge.com

Display and text type set in YWFT Neighborhood
Handlettering by Ellie Erhart
Printed by 1010 Printing International Limited in
   Huizhou, Guangdong, China
Production supervision by Jennifer Most Delaney
Designed by Ellie Erhart

Library of Congress Cataloging-in-Publication Data
Names: Leitner, Inbal, author, illustrator.
Title: The longest, strongest thread / Inbal Leitner.
Description: Watertown, MA: Charlesbridge Publishing, 2022. | "First published
   in Great Britain in 2020 by Scallywag Press, London." | Audience: Ages 3–7. |
   Audience: Grades K–1. | Summary: "A little girl is moving far away and worries
   her grandmother won't be able to find her—but her grandmother explains that
   they are united by a strong thread of love."—Provided by publisher.
Identifiers: LCCN 2021033305 (print) | LCCN 2021033306 (ebook) |
   ISBN 9781623543594 (hardcover) | ISBN 9781632892461 (ebook)
Subjects: LCSH: Grandmothers—Juvenile fiction. | Grandparent and
   child—Juvenile fiction. | Moving, Household—Juvenile fiction. | CYAC:
   Grandmothers—Fiction. | Separation (Psychology)—Fiction. | Moving,
   Household—Fiction.
Classification: LCC PZ7.1.L44455 Lo 2022 (print) | LCC PZ7.1.L44455
   (ebook) | DDC [E]—dc23
LC record available at https://lccn.loc.gov/2021033305
LC ebook record available at https://lccn.loc.gov/2021033306

The Longest, Strongest Thread

INBAL LEITNER

ici Charlesbridge

This suitcase is *so heavy.*

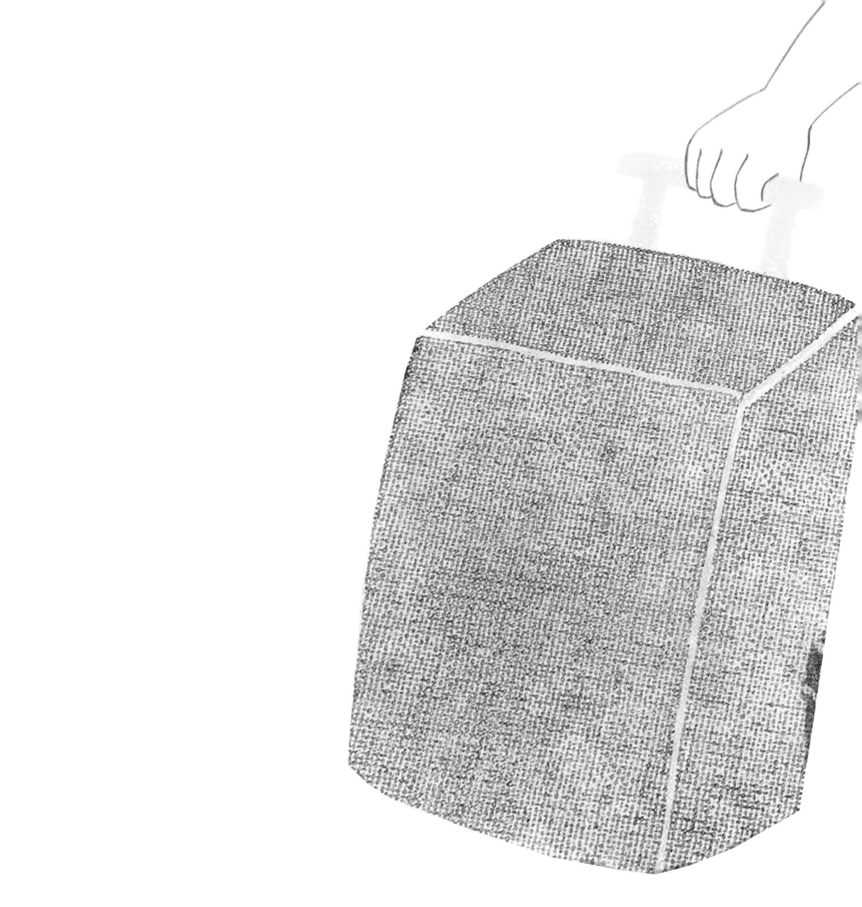

I think I have everything I'll need in my new home
where the lakes freeze in winter.
We are flying there soon.

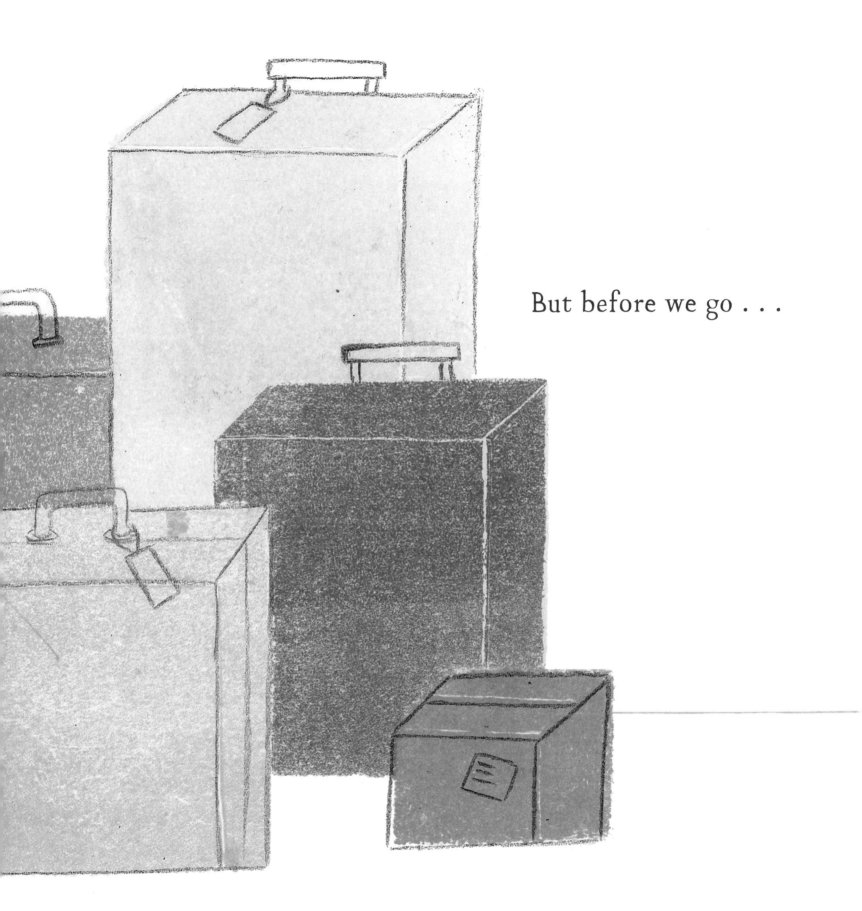

But before we go . . .

. . . I am visiting Grandma to say goodbye.
I wish she could come, too.

She is staying here where it is warm
and she has her sewing studio.

I *love* Grandma's studio.

I help her choose
soft, warm fabric

and the strongest
blue thread.

My new home is very far away.

I must draw Grandma a map so she can find me.

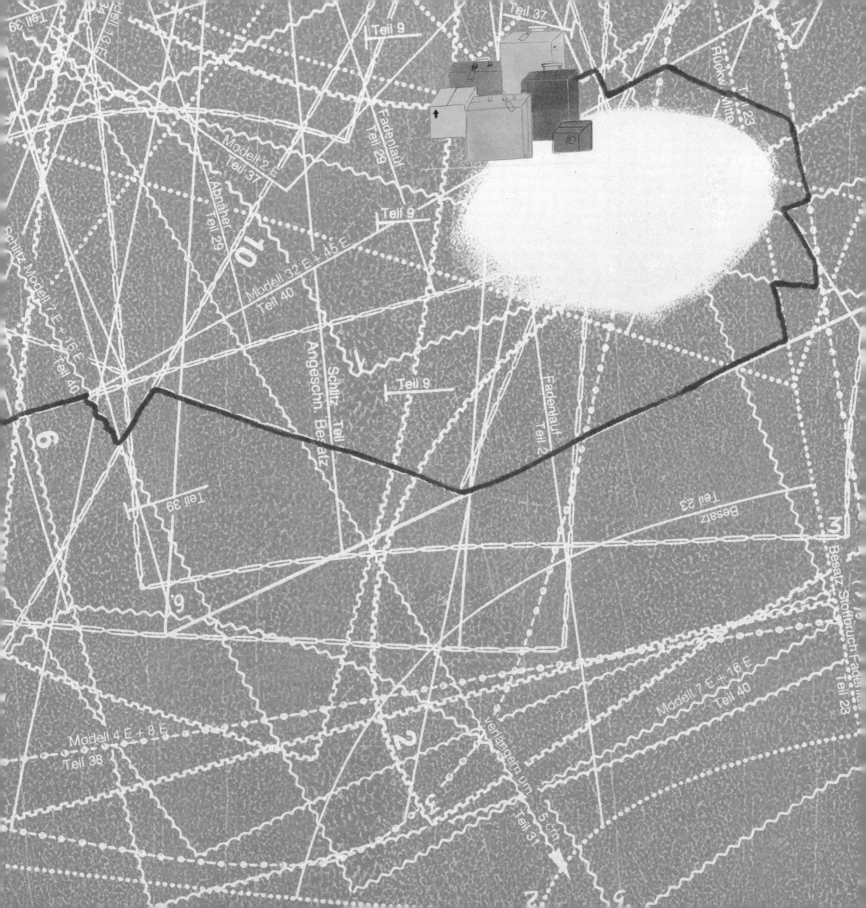

Even if she knows
where I am,

Grandma can't walk
all the way to my
new home.

So I am making her an airplane she can use to fly.

If only there were an enormous magnet I could use to pull her to me whenever I want.

Grandma says I shouldn't worry that
my new home is so very far away.

She says we are connected by the longest,
strongest thread in the whole world.

I love Grandma,

and Grandma
loves me.

We don't want to say goodbye.

But she promises me that when winter comes,
and the lakes freeze . . .

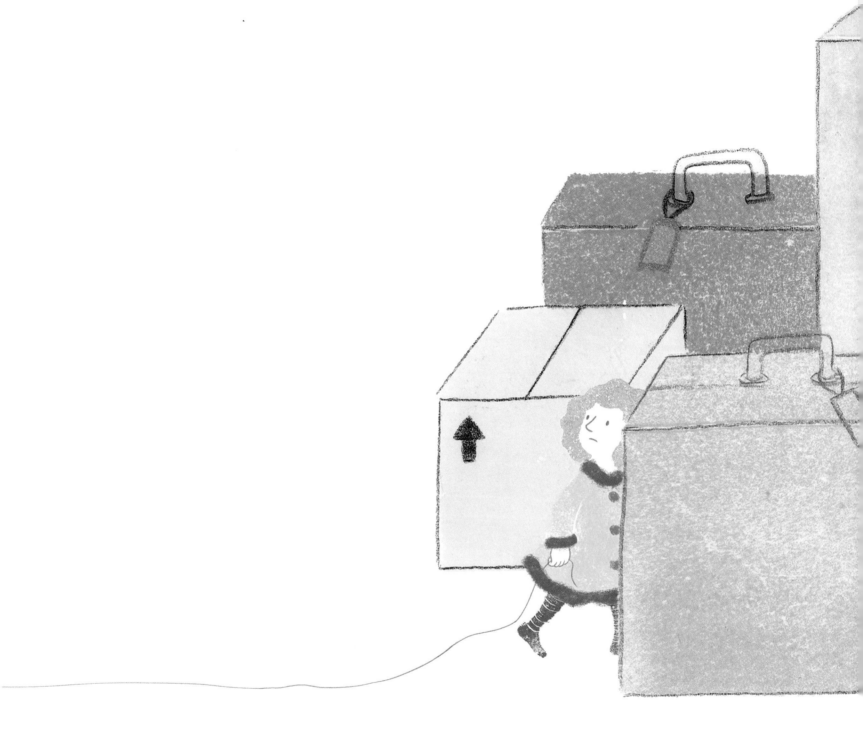

. . . she will surely use the map I gave her
and fly all the way to find me.